This Starfish Bay book belongs to

....

BROWN BEAR CAN'T SLEEP

Yijun CAI

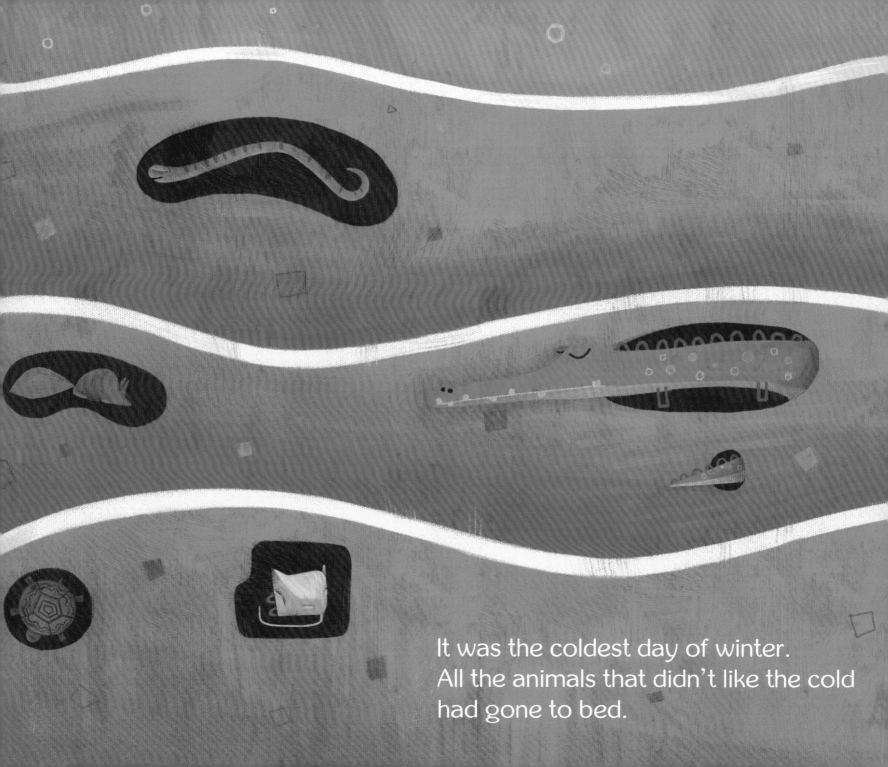

It was the coldest day of winter.
All the animals that didn't like the cold
had gone to bed.

Brown Bear had also gone to bed. But he couldn't fall asleep!
"What should I do?" he wondered.
Staying at home through the long winter was very, very boring.

But if Brown Bear went outside, he would be laughed at by the animals that did like the cold.

Brown Bear needed a plan.

He looked through his books.

The Encyclopedia of Bears

POLAR BEARS are the world's largest bear. They live on land and spend most of their time on the Arctic sea ice. Polar bears are covered in thick white fur, including their ears and paws, and have a little black nose.

Brown Bear had an idea. If he wore a big white sweater and dressed up as a Polar Bear, then he would be able to stay warm, and he wouldn't be laughed at.

Yes, it was a very good idea!

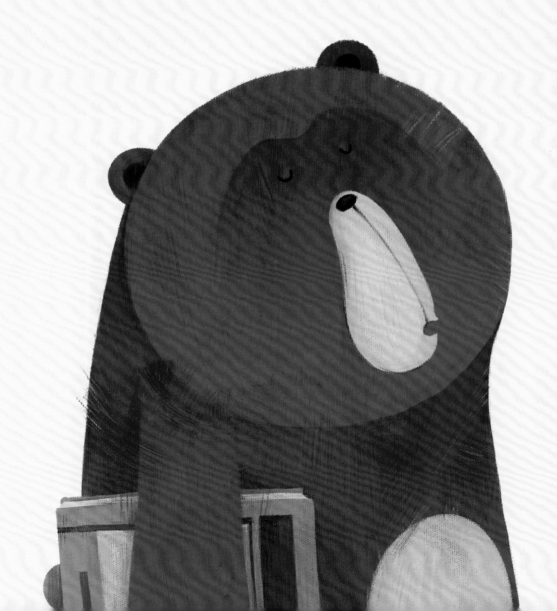

To look like a Polar Bear he needed a huge white sweater.

To make a huge white sweater, Brown Bear needed lots and lots of white wool.
He reached for the phone.
For lots and lots of white wool, he needed …

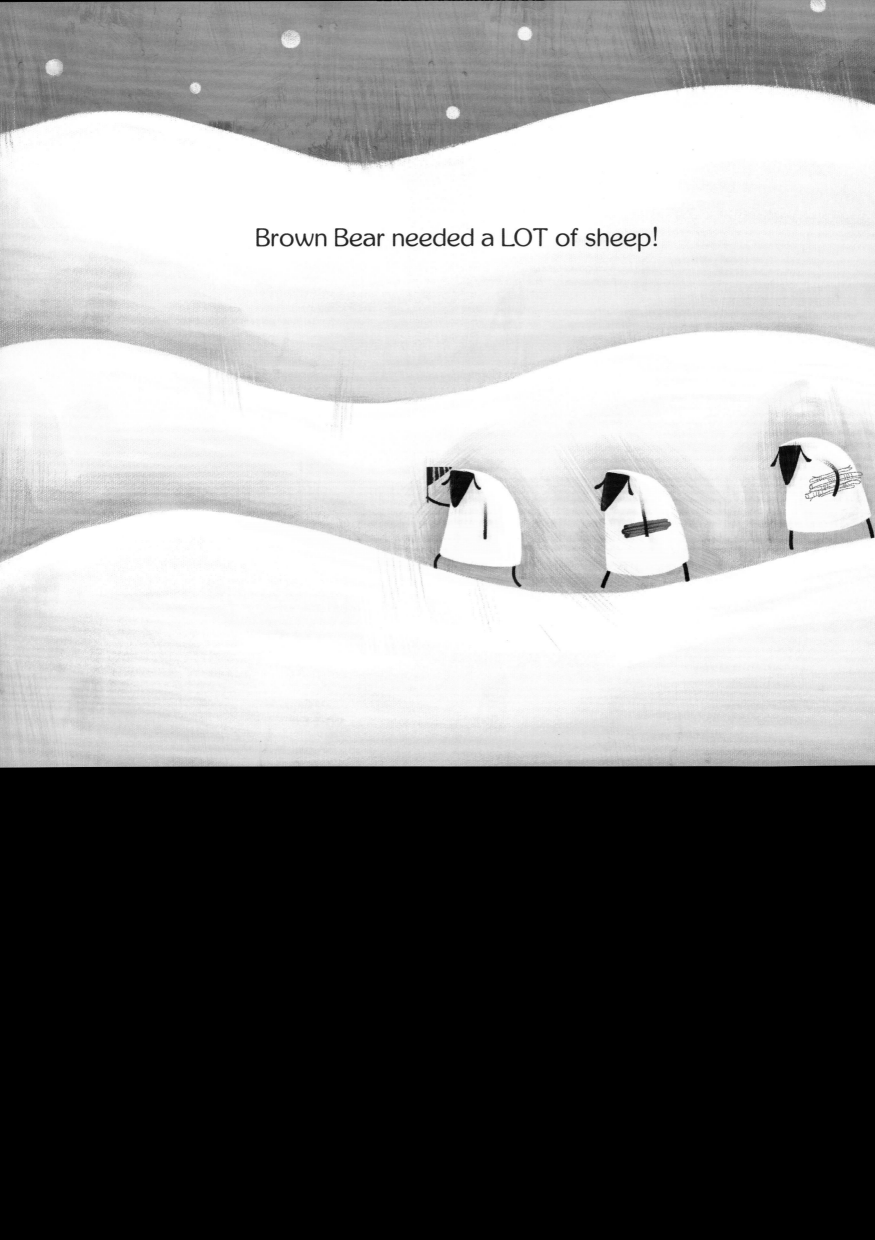

Brown Bear needed a LOT of sheep!

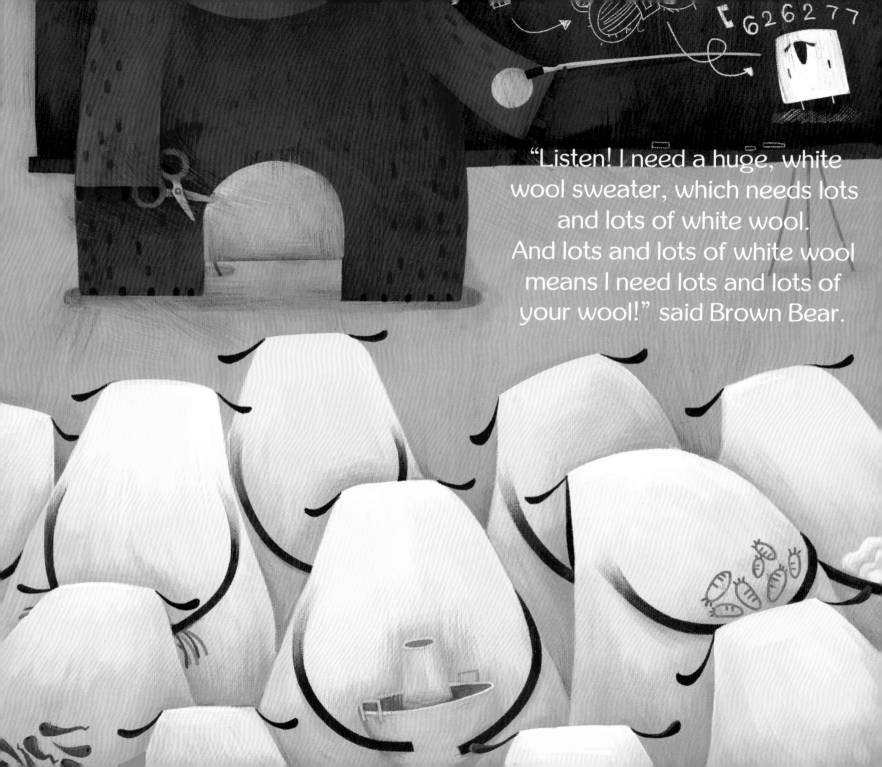

"Listen! I need a huge, white wool sweater, which needs lots and lots of white wool. And lots and lots of white wool means I need lots and lots of your wool!" said Brown Bear.

"Brown Bear, how much
sheep's wool do you need?"
the Sheep asked.

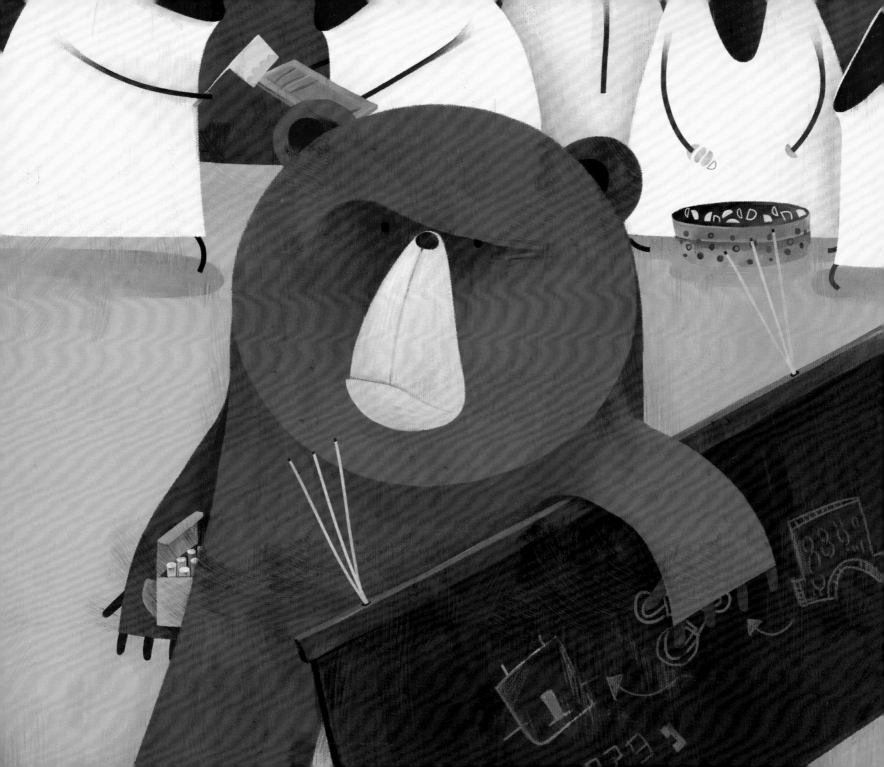

"Hmm! I'll have to think carefully about that!" Brown Bear replied.

He also needed a lot of water to wash the sheep's wool.
After much thought, Mr Brown Bear worked out just the right amount of water.

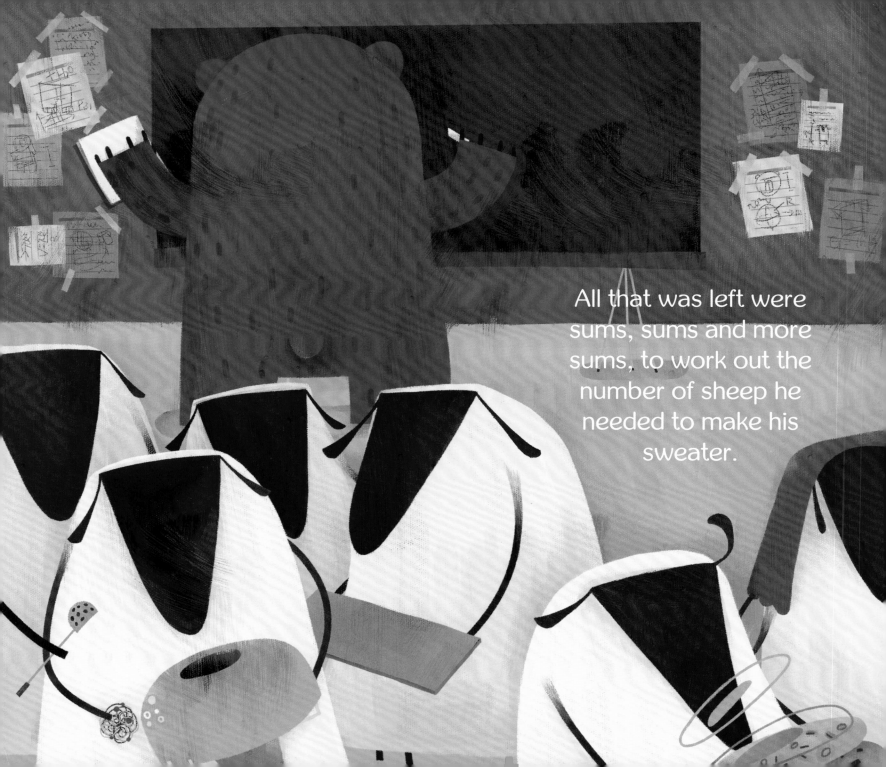

All that was left were sums, sums and more sums, to work out the number of sheep he needed to make his sweater.

"I've got it!"

he shouted at last.
"Quick! Gather round, so that I can
count the sheep!"

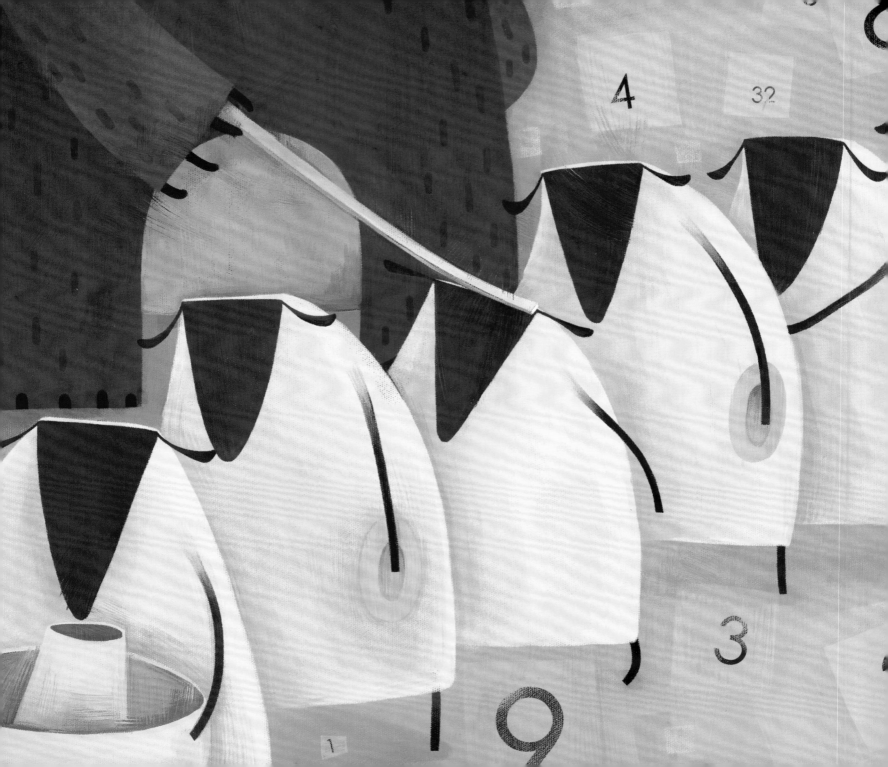

"One sheep… two sheep… three sheep…" he started.

"Sixty sheep..."

Brown Bear yawned.

"Counting sheep is making me sleepy." He yawned again.

Silence! The counting had stopped.
"Let's switch the light off," said the Sheep.
"Goodnight, Brown Bear."

At last, Brown Bear had fallen fast asleep ... just like all the other animals.

STARFISH BAY
CHILDREN'S BOOKS

An imprint of Starfish Bay Publishing
www.starfishbaypublishing.com
STARFISH BAY is a trademark of Starfish Bay Publishing Pty Ltd.

BROWN BEAR CAN'T SLEEP

© Yijun Cai, 2018
ISBN 978-1-76036-048-1
First Published 2018
Printed and bound in China by Beijing Shangtang Print & Packaging Co., Ltd.
11 Tengren Road, Niulanshan Town, Shunyi District, Beijing, China

Sincere thanks to Courtney Chow, Jenny Crowhurst, Belinda Piscino and Gale Winskill (in alphabetical order) from Starfish Bay Children's Books for translating and/or editing this book.
Starfish Bay Children's Books would also like to thank Elyse Williams for her creative efforts in preparing this edition for publication.

Yijun Cai is a freelance illustrator who now resides in Hangzhou, China. She often draws her inspiration from curious thoughts. One winter night, she wondered, "When humans can't sleep, we try all sorts of methods to make ourselves fall asleep. What about bears?" And that is how *Brown Bear Can't Sleep* was born.